MONTVILLE TWP. PUBLIC LIBRARY
90 Horseneck Road
Montville, N.J. 07045

W9-AQB-986

0 1021 0177905 0

ON LINE

Text copyright © 2004 by Kathleen W. Deady
Illustrations copyright © 2004 by Linda Bronson

All rights reserved. International copyright secured. No part of this book may be reproduced, stored in a retrieval system, or transmit-
ted in any form or by any means—electronic, mechanical, photocopying, recording, or otherwise—without the prior written permission
of Carolrhoda Books, Inc., except for the inclusion of brief quotations in an acknowledged review.

Carolrhoda Books, Inc.
A division of Lerner Publishing Group
241 First Avenue North
Minneapolis, MN 55401 U.S.A.

Website address: www.carolrhodabooks.com

Library of Congress Cataloging-in-Publication Data

Deady, Kathleen W.
  All year long / by Kathleen W. Deady ; illustrations by Linda
Bronson.
        p. cm.
Summary: A rhyming celebration of the cycles of the seasons and the
beauty of the natural world.
  ISBN: 1-57505-537-6 (lib. bdg. : alk. paper)
  1. Seasons—Fiction. 2. Stories in rhyme.] I.
Bronson, Linda, ill. II. Title.
  PZ8.3.D3413lae 2004
  [E]—dc21   2003004520

Manufactured in the United States of America
1 2 3 4 5 6 – JR – 09 08 07 06 05 04

0 1021 0177905 0

8/2004
BWI
$ 15.95

To Ellen Stein, for believing in this book
–K. W. D.

For F. H. B.
–L. B.

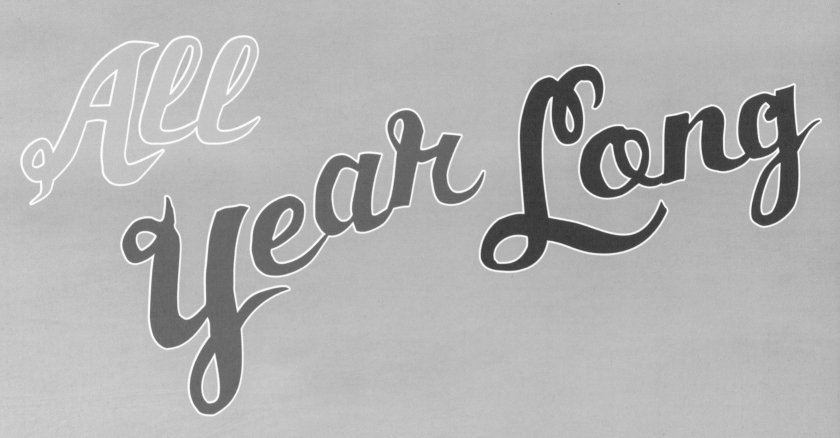

All Year Long

by Kathleen W. Deady

illustrations by Linda Bronson

Carolrhoda Books, Inc./Minneapolis

I know it's spring when robins sing,
and tulips give a nod,

When grass grows green,
and bass are seen on Daddy's fishing rod.

When Mama plants her garden,
and rains go rushing by,

Then quickly comes the sun,

and a rainbow paints the sky.

But just as spring gets started, and I pause to smell the day,

A butterfly flutters by, and summer's on its way.

It's
summer
when the
sidewalk's hot,
and
Mama's garden
grows,

And ice cream cools each day I spend with sand between my toes.

When campfires light the dark of night,
and Daddy plays a song,

While Mama sings a lullaby,
the summer days are long.

Then slowly come the winds of fall,
the days grow short and cool,

And Mama says, "A sweater, please," and, "No more swimming pool."

The leaves of yellow, gold, and red,
ripe pumpkins on the vine,

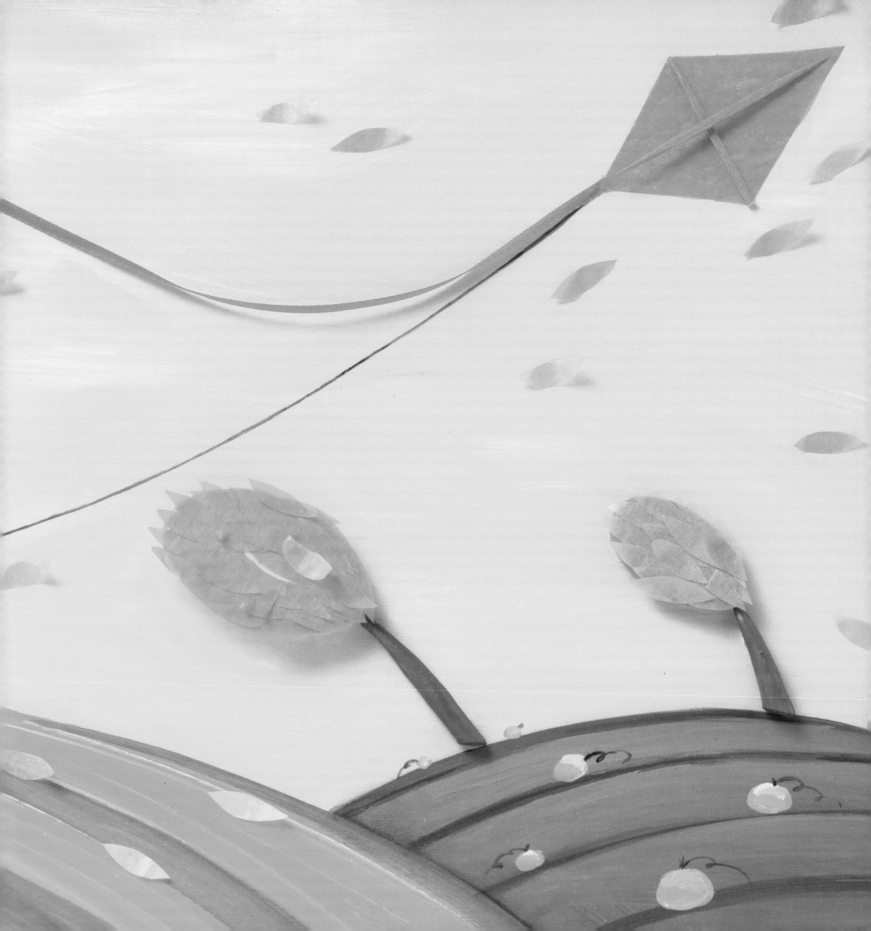

Spooky goblins, scary ghosts,
and witches are a sign

That soon I'll see my breath
and feel the chill of frosty ground.

Then suddenly it's winter...
fluffy snow falls all around!

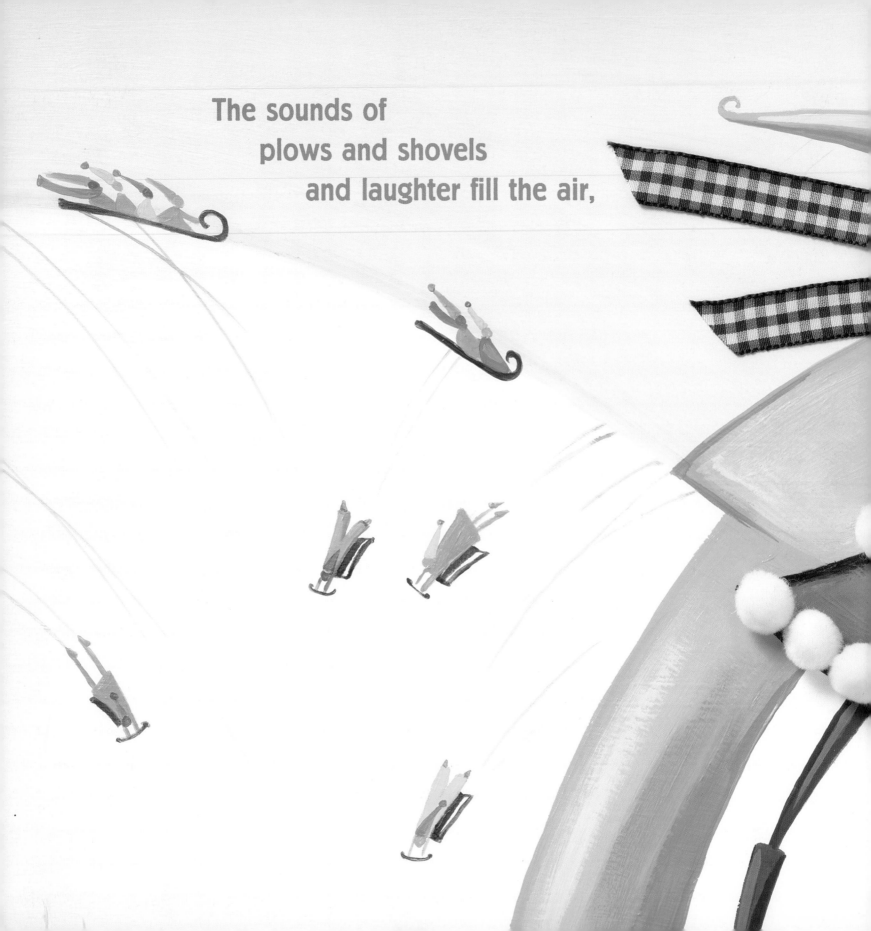

The sounds of
plows and shovels
and laughter fill the air,

As Daddy
helps build snowmen,
and sleds glide everywhere.

But Mama's cocoa keeps us warm
from winter until spring,

When, if I listen closely...

I'll hear a robin sing.

MONTVILLE TWP. PUBLIC LIBRARY
90 Horseneck Road
Montville, N.J. 07045